Mary Queen of Bees

Mary Queen of Bees

Mary [Molly] Wesley Whitelamb [1696–1734]
Sister of John Wesley, founder of the Methodist Church

Epworth, England

DIANE GLANCY

RESOURCE *Publications* · Eugene, Oregon

MARY QUEEN OF BEES
Mary [Molly] Wesley Whitelamb [1696–1734] Sister of John Wesley,
founder of the Methodist Church, Epworth, England

Resource Publications
An Imprint of Wipf and Stock Publishers
199 W. 8th Ave., Suite 3
Eugene, OR 97401

www.wipfandstock.com

PAPERBACK ISBN: 978-1-5326-1765-2
HARDCOVER ISBN: 978-1-4982-4220-9
EBOOK ISBN: 978-1-4982-4249-3

Manufactured in the U.S.A.   MARCH 22, 2017

They compassed me as bees

—PSALM 118:12

I still wake as a child at the head of the stairs in the servant's arms who miss-stepped and we fell down the stairs. Turning my feet under. At my mother's insistence, we were not allowed to cry out. I was quiet as the servant started to fall, unable to catch herself and stop our fall. The servant herself falling over me turning both my feet inward never to walk again without a crutch or a sister on either side. I cried when the pain hit at the bottom of the stairs. Unable to stop my howling.

We weren't allowed to do anything that wasn't church. We were his lambs as he was Lamb. The wool of the Lord was a fire to me.

Our mother taught us to read and write so we could study scripture, but what could we do with it? Teach it to our own daughters who themselves would be a garden surrounded by a wall, shut up with no outlet as we had none? Or as a governess, providing others with knowledge they too could hold inside?

Why this learning if all we were to do was to have children? Our mother, Susanna, held church services for us when our father was in debtor's prison. She didn't like the locum he hired to preach in his place. Soon others came to her services. Crowds gathered in our house on Sunday afternoons to hear Susanna Wesley read her husband's old sermons. During the week, she taught our school lessons. It always felt like Sunday.

I put salt grains on my tongue to sting it. For words not spoken that I wanted to speak. In-between the conjugation of verbs, I wanted to by-pass them and not give them thought.

What did I want to give voice? Not the hymns my mother insisted upon. I did not feel like singing. I hated the sound of my voice. It had no song in it. Why force it? Why make a tongue to sing? It brought me humbly before the Lord. I would not be a song-bird on the branch of a tree that constantly sang to Him. To give praise and thanksgiving. My scrawny voice thin as the blanket that covered us at night.

Her stomach big with another child. Why so many? Couldn't we do with less? I think they heard me. As many infants died as lived. I cried in misery, quietly to myself. I wished them dead so I could have a corner of the bed. A piece of the quilt. So I could have a chair at the table. So I could have bread. And what would we do as women? Marry and have children.

If the dead ones had names I didn't know them. They were born. They cried. They stopped crying. Sometimes they were born without crying. Jedidiah was one of the names.

My body jumped in bed before I slept. I was in the servant's arms at the top of the stairs about to fall. My sisters mocked me. You would think children would have mercy, but they do not. They continued to taunt.

Sometimes there was thunder.

We heard rain. If you cover your head it is warmer. If you leave your stockings on in bed.

The smell of sickness. Vomiting. Running bowels. Brothers and sisters everywhere. It was our job to clean them. The servant could only do so much. IF YOU'RE GETTING SICK, GET OUT OF BED SO WE DON'T HAVE TO PULL OFF SHEETS AND COVERS AND CLEAN THE WHOLE BED. Pulling the mattress out to air. Dragging it down and up the stairs.

THROW UP ON THE FLOOR. Not in the middle of the bed.

I pinched Hetty when she made her body jump, making fun of me. As we were not allowed to cry, I pinched her again. She hit back on the sore places on my feet and I cried out.

STOP. STOP. I'LL COME WITH THE ROD.

I stifled my voice in the covers.

Everlasting children. Nineteen of Samuel and Susanna Wesley. Nine died in infancy.

Samuel b 1690

Emilia (Emily) b 1692

Annesley b 1694 (died)

Jedediah b 1694 (died)

Susanna (Sukey) b 1695

Mary (Molly) b 1696

Mehetabel (Hetty) b 1697

Infant b 1698 (stillborn)

Infant b 1698 (stillborn)

John b 1699 (died)

Benjamin b 1700 (died)

Infant b 1701 (died)

Infant b 1701 (died)

Anne b 1702

John b 1703

Infant b 1705 (accidentally smothered)

Martha (Patty) b 1706

Charles b 1707

Kezzia (Kezzie) b 1709

At times, I was almost warm between Emily and Hetty. Sukey had her own cot at the foot of the bed. On the coldest nights, she got in bed with us. We hardly could move or one of us would fall out. Often they put me at the open edge of the bed. More than once, I was pushed out, and laid shivering on the floor until I climbed onto the cot at the foot of the bed, and thought of the burning wool of the Lord,

We played with the thistle-heads the women used to card the wool after the sheep were sheared. Once Emily ripped the thistle from my hand and left splinters. My mother soaked my hand in water and removed them with a sewing needle.

I would have made a doll from twigs and scraps of old material. Or twigs and leaves. But we weren't allowed. I would have made an apron for the doll from a page in one of my father's books. Tied with thread loose from a binding. He wouldn't have known.

The rod was frequent in the house with so many children full of unmet needs. To do without and not complain, even as small children with fretting always in the eyes, running down the nose.

Conquer the will and bring them to an obedient broken spirit.

When the will of a child is totally subdued, and it is brought to revere and stand in awe of the parents, then a great many childish follies, and faults may be past over.

I insist upon conquering the will of children early because this is the only strong and rational foundation of a religious education. Without this both precept and example will be ineffectual. But when this is thoroughly done, then a child is capable of being governed by the reason and piety of the parents.

They were quickly made to understand they might have nothing they cried for.

—FROM THE WRITINGS OF SUSANNA WESLEY

We could not ask for anything. We ate what was given to us. Even if we gagged. We were regimented. Orderly. Stifled. I wanted to scream out. I kept the screams in the barn inside my head. Between my ears. Oh, they were fondly there. Until I could in the woods by myself cry out, holding along the fence. Until a farmer arrived wondering who was hollering. What was happening? Nothing, sir. I'm just letting out the screams pent up in me. Wild beasts they are. Trampling me at night. I cannot run from them. I cannot walk without my crutch. It isn't a proper crutch. Just a stick a neighbor found and gave to me when he saw me hobbling along the road.

Was there anyone who walked on a crutch in the Bible?

Yes, there were many cripples that Jesus healed.

Any of the disciples or close followers? I asked my mother.

No, but I would learn to walk without help, she said. Or I could lean forever on my sisters.

Jesus hasn't healed me.

Have patience, she said.

There was nothing. Nothing I could do. They laughed at me. Made fun. I was held in derision. A word I heard my father use when he talked of the way neighbors held his views. Because they didn't accept my father's political views. Because he was a zealot. Because he didn't know how to run a farm. Because he didn't pay his bills. Because we were poor. Because his judgement was in want. Because his wife would not let their children play with others.

It is the word, frustration, I ponder. Frustrated. What does it teach me? How to conjugate? No, frustration is more of an object that will not move. It has rooted itself in my being. It is a brilliant needle sparkling in the sun as I sit by the window and sew another patch on my ragged dress. The thread is a line. I could swallow it and choke. I could die and my mother would sweep my shadow from the corner.

A list of what I like—

A corner of our small pasture when no one is there.

The cows because they don't concern themselves with anything but grass. Though sometimes they stare when I pass and share with them the gospel.

The barn. When I am alone there. After milking when my fingers cramp.

The stars when they are bees in the hive of the night sky.

My feet hurt when it rains. They hurt in frost. They know they might become frozen. They do not fit into shoes. They are susceptible to blisters and little rebellions. I would leave my feet in the slaughter pen. Maybe then I could walk.

It is a sin to be morbid. It is a sin not to walk.

Our parents. A mismatched pair. Mother should have been father, and father, mother.

There is a list of what not to do. It is long as forever. All flogged by longings.

She teaches us to read. To want. To long for, by the large writing of my hand.

Therein is the multiplicity of longing.

It is all the same. Suffering. Suffering. The God we belong to requires it. Mother sees to it. Father in his distance does also. He gives us his absence. His inability to handle what needs to be handled.

Our mother meets with all the children once a week. For an hour, she sits before us. Not altogether. But one by one. It is like talking to a cow in the field that looks solemnly at me. Why doesn't she ask what I feel? Why doesn't she say she will stop my sisters from mocking the way I walk? She asks only of my learning of scripture. My slowness. My unworthiness before the Lord. Did she play children when she was child?

But somewhere in the slowness, there is a spark of determination. Maybe it is anger. A pollen to go with the sting. I feel capable of learning. Of being upright before the Lord. Of walking the way others walk—even though it would not be in this lifetime.

My Letters to Paradise—
I would like to not be thwarted at every turn. Even for the most ordinary thing. I would like a soothing for the longing that is a bee sting. I would like for there to be an end to want.

My father worked continually on a commentary of the Old Testament book of Job—*Dissertationes in Librum Jobi.* My youngest sister, Kezzia, was named after one of the daughters of Job [Job 42:14]. Job with seven sons and three daughters. My father with seven daughters and three sons. My father's book was in Latin and Greek, Hebrew, Chaldean and others. Why didn't he just say in English, Job struggled to walk on two feet? To not limp through his trials. Why did my father have to make his work so laborious and ornate? Why couldn't he meet Job where he was? And where was Uz where Job lived? My father posited. Somewhere. Somewhere. He raised more questions than he answered. I feared my father's writing was difficult. No one else seemed to take an interest. The sale of subscriptions was not going well.

Job had to listen to his friends. Eliphaz, Bildad and Zophar. I had my sisters, Emily, Sukey and Hetty. Even the younger ones sometimes taunted me.

My father read all Hebrew texts about Job. No one knows who wrote the book, but my father insisted it was Job himself, standing apart from himself, outside himself, as though he were the character he was writing about. Job knows the earth, the weather, its cycles.

We are gifted with free will, my father tells me, which includes the choice of sin. But I don't know what he connects that thought to.

1701—In a time of prayer my parents argued. My brothers and sisters looked at them startled. She would not say amen to his prayer for King James. The parents were doing what the children could not. We all left the room. I sat on the top stair and listened. My sisters hid in the bed. Finally, the strain broke and my father left the house. The mother sent all the children to bed where we cried softly into our worn blankets.

The following year, my father returned. He was visiting a sick parishioner when the parsonage caught fire, burning all but a third of the house, including his work on the book of Job.

1702—The Fire Number One. Possibilities—[I heard my father say].

Sparks from a neighbor's chimney on our thatch.

Sparks from our own chimney.

A broken chimney tile.

A cracked stove pipe.

A stray ember from the fireplace onto a frayed rug.

The Epworth Rectory had three stories. Made of timber and plaster. Covered with straw thatch. There were seven rooms, kitchen and parlor, hall and buttery. Three large upper rooms where we slept. The house was dim even in the day. At night, a candle hardly made a difference. Outside there was a garden with a stone wall. A barn of timber and clay walls covered with thatch. Three acres beyond the barn that bordered wildness and boredom.

Whatever the cause, the roof, on fire, fell on our bed. The sisters ran from the room. A servant came and led Hetty and me downstairs and pushed us from a window. Why didn't she leave me upstairs? She could have let me die. I would have gone to the Lord that couldn't possibly be worse than the Wesley house.

Our mother was burned on her hands, neck and arms, rushing through the house, trying to find what she could save until the flames would have roasted her. And she fled.

Some of us were sent to live with an uncle while the rectory was rebuilt.

When we were together again, my father took up his work on Job. My mother took up our lessons.

1705—Now our father in debtor's prison. How could we be in debt? We had bought nothing. I never will marry a clergyman. Probably I never will marry.

My mother is overwhelmed with work. When she gives birth, she sends the infant to a neighbor to care for. In the night, the woman rolls over and smothers it. I hear the woman weeping as she comes to my mother with the dead infant in her arms.

My father was a Tory. All Wesley's were conservatives from birth. We had no choice. We were against democratization and reform. My father's politics did not go well. They irritated his parishioners who were illiterate. They were mainly Whigs. They opposed the succession of James, the Duke of York. The congregation also resented my father's prayers for James.

At one point, neighbors burned our flax fields. Later, when my father continued to irritate them, they stabbed our milk cows and called us devils.

The poor pitiful beasts. What had they done?

My Letters to Paradise—
I write to You from this world where poor dumb animals are stabbed. I am haunted by the noise they made. My mother would have told them to be quiet. But I heard their helpless cries. Their misunderstanding of what was happening. The pain of the knife stabbing their thick bodies. How long it took for them to die. I

am sure You are out in the universe holding the formations of the stars. Keeping them in order. But meanwhile on Your earth, there are happenings that need Your attention.

> I never did want bread. But then I had so much care to get it before it was eat, and to pay for it after, as has often made it very unpleasant to me, and I think to have bread on such terms is the next degree of wretchedness to having none at all.
>
> —From the Writings of Susanna Wesley

A Letter from the Wesley Cows in the Field—
It was us who died for them.

My Letters to Paradise—
I am sorry, O Lord, I grieve more for cows than my mother's infants.

In church there was a girl, the only child of her parents. I often saw her walk into the church between them. She sat between her parents also. I looked at her sometimes, unless we sat in the front row, where my father sometimes put us. If I was behind her, I watched her. Once, she turned and looked at me. I didn't look away. I still was wondering what it was like to be the only child in a house.

Once, in despair, thinking the Lord too was an only child— how could he know how I felt in the crowded house where I had to live? But in the night, my arms held tightly to my chest to make room for my sisters, the Lord said to me, you are an only child with me.

1709—The Fire Number Two
We fled the rectory again in the night. Clattering down the stairs. John cried from an upstairs window in the rectory, Help me! Our father, Samuel tried to climb the burning stairs, but could not. He gathered some of us in the garden to pray for our brother's soul, but neighbors made a ladder of hands and shoulders, climbed up and brought him down.

The Dispersement of Children after the Fire.

Once again, we lost nearly everything except the nightclothes we wore. I was thirteen years old. Our mother walked through the flames, this time singeing her hair that stood up in jagged wisps from her head. Afterwards, Uncle Matthew Wesley, my father's brother, a doctor in London, took Sukey and Hetty when we had no place to live. Emily stayed with our mother in the nearby house of a neighbor. I was sent to the neighbor who had smothered my infant brother. Did my mother want her to smother me?

The fire was a blessing. Afterwards, we were scattered to families and friends and talked to servants and ran and played with children.

The woman did not want to smother me after all. She let me sit warmly by the fire. She gave me an old umbrella I patched. I stood in the rain at the backdoor and listened to the clumping of the drops.

Someone showed me a picture of a rolling chair, Spain, 1595. I dreamed I had a little chair with wheels and could spin here and there. But how would it get up the stairs to the girls' room where I slept, and sat sometimes during the day?

When the house was rebuilt after the fire, the custom of singing psalms morning and evening resumed. My mother also read a psalm for the day, and chapters in the New Testament and the Old Testament, after which we said our private prayers.

The harsh discipline returned in the rectory once again. I welcomed it. I sanctioned it. I longed for it. I hated it.

Not one child after a year old was heard to cry aloud.

—From the Writings of Susanna Wesley

Mother's lesson.

Ahaz was a wicked king. He made his sons pass through the fire—II Kings 16:3. What did that mean? We asked our mother. Was it like our own father who prayed for John after being unable to rescue him? Did it mean we all passed through the fire when our house burned? Some questions our mother did not answer.

She allowed us only to ask questions she thought we should ask. Otherwise she ignored what we said.

Did it mean we passed through fire when hungry? When sick? When crippled? When crowded with other sisters in the same bed? When burning inside with longing? When burning with more than one longing? Or with a longing that branched like a tree with leaves falling when we lay in bed at night and smelled the stench the fire left in the parsonage? But with it also, the smell of new thatch.

Ahaz saw the holy furniture of the tabernacle, my mother said—the laver, lampstand, table of bread, and other pieces. He had his priest, Urijah, made similar furniture. Only Ahaz rearranged the pieces. He made offerings to God in the wrong places. He cut off borders, and took the laver from the oxen that were under it, and put it on the pavement of stones—II Kings 16:17.

There was not a multiplicity of worlds in the Lord. He was single in heart. This is what our mother said. We were wrong to want our own way. It always would be wrong. It was humanity's way.

Outside, the birds were screeching. It meant the cat was in the tree, or a bird not of their kind was encroaching. Maybe it was my own evil thoughts that would pervert the words of the Lord like Ahaz.

This was the pain. If I could, I would dismantle what belonged to the Lord like Ahaz, and use it in my own way. I would be like my father. He didn't have a head for cattle. He didn't know the fields. He was overwhelmed by the children Susanna gave him. He couldn't handle the numbers of us. He didn't know how to handle our lives. He had dreams that scoured him. The neighbors were against him. His own congregation. His wife. His children. The world, it seemed, where he could not fit. Or the world was more than he could dwell in. He always thought beyond it. He dreamed of other places. He couldn't pay his bills. He had his books he bought. Nothing we could eat. Nothing we could wear. Impractical. Impractical.

In my despondence I read Psalm 22—My God why have You forsaken me? Why are You so far from helping me? O God, I cry by day, and You do not answer, and by night but find no rest.

Blessed fire. Return. Scatter us to other houses where we might play.

There is something holy about fire. It had its wicked side when it burned houses, but even when it did, there was something holy about it.

After the fire, our father bought travel books and talked of missionary work in China or the East Indies. He worked with his scorched manuscripts on Job. Every page more complicated than the last. He seemed bogged down in possibilities and interpretations. He could not let it go.

Meanwhile we could not go out in society in the shabby clothes we wore. No one would know we studied scripture on our own.

Epworth. Dear Epworth. The ground full of graves of the Wesley infants. Is there any way out of Epworth other than death?

My father planted mulberry, cherry, pear and walnut trees after the fire. It took a year to rebuild the house and left us farther in debt. My mother and a servant planted beans, peas and Brussels sprouts in the garden.

I could crawl as a bee, awkward with its heavy wings. I am silent in this wretched house filled with God. No one hears. Not even God who must be poor also, though He owns cattle, the Bible says—Psalm 50:10.

The Israelites made offerings of animal sacrifice in the Old Testament, but that was before Christ offered himself in the New Testament. Now we make our offerings with the praises of our mouth. I praise You for my bent feet. I praise You for the stiffness of my back. I praise You for prison. I praise You for our father's debt. I praise You for parents that only meet to make more children.

The bees leave in the rain. Not one buzzes around the window. Where do they go? Is there a small bee-house somewhere unseen by the eyes of people who pass with their umbrellas? Or watch from an upstairs window? Is there a small place under the wide petals of flowers? Maybe in the loft of the barn. Or in a hive somewhere when the bees have to stay in and sit at the table and study scripture—probably the reliable book of Job my father reads to us to sober any light-heartedness that might try to wedge itself between the somber layers of our house.

I open the umbrella our neighbor gave me and set it in the garden for the bees to get under.

1716–1717—We begin to hear noises in the parsonage. Rappings. Weird sounds everywhere. We called the ghost, Old Jeffrey. Our father didn't believe us until his trencher, the wooden platter on which he cut the meat for our meal, moved on the table.

Anne Wesley was sent to the attic with her trumpet to scare away Old Jeffrey.

A list of what I like—

> Old Jeffrey, the ghost that haunts the parsonage with noises. Maybe I don't like him as much as I like the mystery of him. Something beyond our poor circumstances. It makes me think of Paradise.

I heartily rejoice at having such an opportunity of convincing myself, past doubt or scruple, of the existence of some beings besides those we see.

—FROM THE LETTER OF AMELIA WESLEY TO JOHN,
HER BROTHER, WHO ASKED HIS FAMILY TO WRITE
OF THEIR EXPERIENCE WITH OLD JEFFREY

In Epworth, at the baker's shop, while carriages passed in the street, there was a fruitcake in the window. I stopped in absolute stillness before the shop. A strange, gummy feeling came over me. I saw the glazed fruit sticking up from the cake. I wanted to taste it. To eat it. To put my fingers into the honey and nuts.

Why don't we ever have anything? I asked.

No one answered.

My mother took my arm and pulled me roughly ahead—away from the baker's shop.

I knew then heaven was a FRUITCAKE. I also knew it was tea and crumpets, gingerbread, mincemeat, shepherd's pie full of potatoes, carrots, lamb and gravy made with heavy cream—a steaming crust covering it like a warm blanket. He gave Himself as a Lamb. My mother dragged me along. I cried with the thought of the fruitcake. She boxed me about the ears, but I kept crying. When I tripped, she did not give me a chance to stand again, but dragged me on my knees until my sisters helped me stand, ripping the sleeve of my shabby coat.

My Letters to Paradise—
I would like a fruitcake. I would eat all of it myself. I would like my father's crops not to fail. I would like my father to think about us as much as he thinks about Job.

In my imagination a letter came to me from Paradise—
On the supper table of the Lord there is fruitcake.
Walking in the flowers, a bee stung my leg above my high-topped shoe. It must have gotten caught under my dress. As I had no leggings, it attached itself to my skin. It must have felt trapped. Nothing to do but sting. My leg throbbed where it stung. How could a small bee inflict such a wounding that continued to hurt?

Church. Church. Always church. The hard wooden pews. The tall windows and ceiling. The arches along the aisles. The hymns. The slow hymns. The drone of them. The bee sting of church. The hurtful slowness. Yet the pollen given. The sweetness of the word. The hum of bee wings. Under their wings I trust. They carried me away. And afterwards, everyone putting on their cloaks and shawls. Picking up their umbrellas. Their voices swarming from the church. Church. Church. Always church.

The noises I hear most frequently—
church bell
fire bell
the cry of an infant downstairs

Here it is, my father left the study of Job for an afternoon, and showed me a passage from the Bible. And Jonathan, Saul's son, had a son that was lame in his feet. He was five years old when the tidings came of [the death of] Saul and Jonathan out of Jezreel, and his nurse took him up, and fled; and it came to pass, as she made haste to flee, that he fell, and became lame. And his name was Mephibosheth—II Samuel 4:4.

I cried for Mephibosheth. I cried that he was lame the rest of his life. I cried that he could not run as he saw children run. That he could not walk without pain.

And there was of the house of Saul a servant whose name was Ziba. And when they had called him unto David, the king said unto him, Art thou Ziba? And he said, Thy servant is he.
And the king said, Is there not yet any of the house of Saul, that I may shew the kindness of God unto him? And Ziba said unto the king, Jonathan hath yet a son, which is lame on his feet.
And the king said unto him, Where is he? And Ziba said unto the king, Behold he is in the house of Machir, the son of Ammiel, in Lo-debar.
Then king David sent, and fetched him out of the house of Machir, the son of Ammiel, from Lo-debar.
Now when Mephibosheth, the son of Jonathan, the son of Saul, was come unto David, he fell on his face, and did reverence. And David said, Mephibosheth. And he answered, Behold thy servant!
And David said unto him, Fear not: for I will surely shew thee kindness for Jonathan, thy father's sake, and will restore thee all the land of Saul thy father; and thou shalt eat bread at my table continually.
And he bowed himself, and said, What is thy servant, that thou shouldest look upon such a dead dog as I am?
Then the king called to Ziba, Saul's servant, and said unto him, I have given unto thy master's son all that pertained to Saul and to all his house.
Thou, therefore, and thy sons, and thy servants, shall till the land for him, and thou shalt bring in the fruits, that thy master's son may have food to eat: but Mephibosheth thy master's son shall eat bread always at my table. Now Ziba had fifteen sons and twenty servants.
Then Ziba said to the king, According to all that my lord the king hath commanded his servant, so shall thy servant do. As for Mephibosheth, said the king, he shall eat at my table, as one of the king's sons.
And Mephibosheth had a young son, whose name was Micha. And all that dwelt in the house of Ziba were servants unto Mephibosheth.
So Mephibosheth dwelt in Jerusalem: for he did eat continually at the king's table; and was lame in both his feet—II Samuel 9:2–13.

I cried until my father left the table, and my mother herself was distraught. I transgressed her rules. I cried and cried calling the name of Mephibosheth. Mephibosheth. Lame in both feet. Unable to walk without help. Recipient of mercy. I sat at the poverty of my table and swallowed my sobs with my small portion of bread.

I was unable to leave the table with the lumps of soggy bread in my stomach. Squeezed into tight little balls. I sorrowed. I sorrowed. Emily and Sukey pulled me from the table.

Mephibosheth. I sobbed. If I had a doll, I would name her that.

My list of longings—

I would eat continually at the king's table.

I would not be a dead dog.

If I ever had a child, I would name her Mephibosheth.

Our father was in debt again. He was a Tory, and when the Whigs were in power, they cut his funding. His politics were unwelcome. He would not be quiet about them. An impractical man in any circumstance.

The cows moan from the field. Uncle Matthew Wesley, our father's brother, sent money for one of the cows. A neighbor gave us another. Or maybe one cow had survived the stabbing. I heard an owl howl from the tree. The rooster is awake. The stars cry out. Or is it my own voice? No, it is not mine. I would be struck for my insolence—the first of which would be—crying out at the unlistening God. He lets us crawl on the earth and does not care. I cannot question. I only can believe and say nothing. Let Him walk on feet that won't carry his legs. Let Him feel the hurt. Let Him want to run but cannot. Let Him get hit with my mother's stick.

If I had a proper dress, I could go to meetings where they talk of books and the ideas in them. I could meet with people. I could speak. I could hear their thoughts. I would keep my feet under the hem of my dress. But to spend another stifling afternoon stuck inside myself. Are my brothers and sisters the only ones in the world?

I could catch a steamer to another land. Now I would be like my father always planning mission trips when he has no money.

It is our forbidden city. This house in which we live. Rebuilt from fire. Sparse as a mowed field.

My sisters have names taken from their own. Or they were given to them, rather. Amelia is Emily. Susanna is Sukey. I, Mary, am Molly. Mehetabel is Hetty. Anne is sometimes Annie. Martha is Patty. Kezzia is Kezzie. Only the boys, Samuel, John and Charles go by their given names.

We, the girls, are spilling over in the house with our bodies growing taller every day. You are crowding me. Move! How can we fit in this bed? FINALLY, some of the sisters will be grown and can leave. That is what we wait for. More space in the bed. More room at the table. Another crust of bread to eat. We would swallow it all ourselves, but we must share.

Emily as the oldest girl is the first to go. She is leaving for Uncle Matthew's house in London, but becomes ill. Smallpox keeps her with us. A deadly disease. It passes over her. My mother puts her on a cot in the kitchen. She cannot sleep in the bed with us. We would push her from the upstairs window. Lest her disease spread to us. It is Uncle Matthew's order from London, who is a physician.

The smallpox has been very mortal at Epworth most of this summer. Our family have all had it besides me, and I hope God will preserve me from it, because your father can't yet very well spare money to bury me.

—FROM THE WRITINGS OF SUSANNA WESLEY
[TO JOHN WESLEY]

While Emily lay moaning and turning on her cot, the dancing teacher comes to the house. My mother is not all grief. We could not go to the dancing teacher's house because it would not become the minister's daughters. When the dancing teacher is at our house, my mother plays the rickety piano. I sit in the chair moving my legs. The chair is my dance partner. Emily stays on her cot in the kitchen because the room is warmer. The fire could be kept going in the stove. The draftiness is not as drafty in a corner of the kitchen. And so the sisters, Sukey, Hetty, Anne, Patty, twirl and turn in the room. Kezzie still young enough she falls at nearly every turn. Even the drizzle outside the window seems to fall with glee. I suspect my mother wishes to thwart the moroseness in the straw and timber of the house. Or at least the oppressiveness I feel.

When the smallpox sores heal on Emily's face and chest, she leaves for Uncle Matthew's house.

Our father also spends the winter in London. His work. His research. His friendships are there. He raises more debt than anything. We hardly have clothes in Epworth to cover our bodies. The wardrobe in our room is empty. Nothing hanging in it. Only dresses hanging there when we have on our night clothes. In the morning, we put on the same dresses with aprons over them to keep them clean. Our want is upmost in our prayers.

It is our responsibility to teach the younger sisters. I spend many hours with Hetty, then Anne. They are not as interested in study as I, who could do nothing else. I often thought how hard it must be for my father with his rough and unlearned parishioners at Epworth. No wonder he always wanted to be someplace else. Often, I stayed in our father's library with his books. On Sundays, the locums came to preach in his absence.

If Emily saw our father in London, her letters did not say so. Meanwhile, in the rectory at Epworth, we slept and woke and ate and studied.

Emily planned on becoming a governess. She liked being with Uncle Matthew, a Dissenter, who was not fond of the rigid Anglicanism of his brother, Samuel, who is our father. Emily wrote that Uncle Matthew was glad she was more open-minded than her father.

There came other letters from Emily. Robert Leybourne was his name. A man she met. She was in love. She would have continued in Uncle Matthew's house, but was unable to find governess work. She returned to Epworth, where she continued to write to Leybourne.

Samuel, our brother, disliked him. He told our mother to end the relationship. Emily was devastated. She spent hours over the letters to Leybourne. After three years, our mother finally broke it off. Leybourne did nothing. Emily spent many days looking from the window in our father's study.

> That dismal winter I shall ever remember: my mother was sick, confined to her bed, my father in danger of arrests every day [for indebtedness]. I had a large family to keep, and a small sum to keep it on; expecting my mother's death every day, and my father's confinement; and yet in all this care, the loss of Leybourne was heaviest. For near half a year I never slept half a night, and, now, provoked at all my relations, resolved never to marry.

> —FROM A LETTER OF AMELIA [EMILY] WESLEY
> TO JOHN WESLEY

It was hard to walk in the street where people were scarred with smallpox. My younger sisters stared until I pulled them sharply ahead. That's what Christianity is, I decided. A staring ahead. A moving forward without letting side-visions interfere. There was nothing here to hold my interest. But hope. Or the muddle of pointless thoughts, some of which became faith, which became substance. I knew to hold onto faith. To Christianity. That strange, unfathomable religion that held its believers in bondage. But I had my mother still pounding her lessons into my head.

I could do nothing by myself. It seemed I could do nothing with Christ but hold on as he held on. In scripture, he said he could do nothing but what the father told him to do. It took great strength to hold onto nothing. It was willful as those horses I saw in the streets of Epworth. I could do nothing without Christ. I was dependent. Alone in a house with others. Christianity was a separation into one's self where I stood alone, even when tight against my sisters. Christianity was a journey while standing in one place. Not moving from the house though I longed to go. Christianity was a longing. Why did the hymns go on and on about blessed hope? I felt no renewal. But determination in the struggle to stand upright.

This is the map of the Wesley house. My father at work. My mother with children, though she had servants and spent time by herself in her room. My older sisters pining. Uncle Matthew in London. Samuel, John and Charles at school.

When Emily heard of a teaching position at a boarding school in Lincoln, she applied. She was there until the school disbanded five years later. Then Emily was persuaded to return to Epworth instead of looking for another position. She came back with dresses to hang in the wardrobe, until life with father took her money and she had to sell her clothes. She saw the unending poverty of the family, though they told her life at Epworth had improved to persuade her to return.

Eventually, Emily accepted a teaching position at another boarding school in Lincoln. When our mother, Susanna, was ill, Emily returned, and thereafter started her own school at Gainsborough when our mother recovered.

I have a fairer prospect at Gainsborough even than I could hope for; my greatest difficulty will be want of money at my first entrance. I shall furnish my school with canvas, worsteds, silks, etc. etc. and am much afraid of being dipped in debt at first; but God's will will be done! Troubles of that kind are what I have been used to. Will you lend me the other three pounds, which you designed for me at Lady Day? [March 25th the Feast of Annunciation] It would help me much. You will if you can, am sure, for so I would do by you.

—FROM THE LETTERS OF AMELIA [EMILY] WESLEY
TO JOHN WESLEY

I studied the Bible. What else could I do? I had been taught the foundations of a Christian education—stillness and obedience. I never could be a scholar like my father. I don't think he made progress either, but seemed to hover over Job finding constant trails through the chapters that took him on many journeys through what must be a straighter book. It seemed to me anyway.

Often, I was back reading Mephibosheth, the lame son of Jonathan, David's friend. One morning, I started with another verse— the one before the nurse fleeing with Mephibosheth in her arms. And the Beerothites fled to Gittaim and were sojourners there to this day—II Samuel 4:3. BEE-rothites? The BEE-ROTHITES were in the Bible! They buzzed around a servant's head to make her fall. With an infant who didn't know she was in her last moments with feet that were not broken. Mauled by bees. Mutilated. Was there no end of my anger? My mother did not allow that voice to surface, but it was there. Its eyes glowed red. Its toenails curled under. They were hard to cut. Impossible. Hold still, Molly, my mother said.

I knew it was Beer-o-thites. I did not care. I called them Beerothites. People of the bees. I was one of them. My stinger of wrath was that I was crippled and nothing could be done. I could be turned out to become a beggar. I'd seen them in town. My mother hurried past as they called out to us. We didn't have coins to give them. I would have swallowed them myself if we did. No, I would have bought fruitcake in the shop window.

There go the ragged Wesley's. Beggars themselves. They are in a house so crowded love could not grow. Only survival. As plants overcrowded in a garden bend and twist their way toward sunlight, out of necessity smothering those closest to them.

In the anger of my delirium I wanted to say—

Job fell down the stairs as an infant and was crippled thereafter. He stopped in Bee-roth. I wanted to unravel the text. I wanted to rearrange what it said. To make it more agreeable. Less unravelling to my life.

I found another reference—Beeroth, a city of Benjamin when territory was portioned to the tribes of Israel—Joshua 18:25. Mephibosheth visited him often.

Joshua in the promised land divided the land unto the children of Israel—Joshua 18:10.

And to Molly [Mary] Wesley he gives broken feet and a slow journey. To Mephibosheth a cup of tea.

I am coming, Father Abraham, may your grace and will be abundant in our lives. Amen.

My Letters to Paradise—
I look forward to thee, New Jerusalem. Where all wounds are healed. I will remember no more the stories of the servant girl who tripped on the stairs and fell with me. No, she fell upon me. My body broke her fall. I hardly was more than an infant and cannot remember why she fell. She was not paying attention. She miss-stepped. It is easy to do. Once in a while I heard a brother or sister fall on the hard stairs. I wanted to call out. Be careful or you will be crippled like me. I wanted to put a sign at the head of the stairs. Beware from one who has fallen here. I wanted to put markings on the wall where I fell as a memorial to my fall. Sometimes when I walked down the stairs holding onto the rail, I remembered tumbling. I think I remembered tumbling. No, I don't remember tumbling.

> . . . but since God has cut me off from the pleasurable parts of life, and rendered me incapable of attracting the love of my relations, I must use my utmost endeavor to secure an eternal happiness, and he who is no respector of persons will require no more than he has given. You may not think that I am uncharitable in blaming my relations for want of affection, and I should readily agree with you had I not convincing reasons to the contrary; one of which, and I think an undeniable one, is this, that I have always been the jest of the family—and it is not I alone who make this observation, for then it might very well be attributed to my suspicion—but here I will leave it . . .
>
> —MARY [MOLLY] WESLEY, LETTER TO HER BROTHER,
> JOHN WESLEY, C. 1720

It hurt to sit for long. It hurt to stand. I was reading the Bible—

And Mephibosheth, the son of Saul, came down to meet the king and had neither dressed his feet, nor trimmed his beard, nor washed his clothes, from the day the king departed until the day he came again—II Samuel 19:24–30.

Both Saul and David had sons named Mephibosheth? Or was it one Mephibosheth, the son of Jonathan, the son of Saul? I had trouble with the Bible. It was hard to understand. There were little trippings between verses. Unclarities. Confusions.

My Letters to Paradise—
I will not dress my feet until the king returns. I will not hide my feet in rags wrapped around my toes. I would like toenails that do not grow. I would like not to have crooked toes. At least I get the shoes my older sisters outgrew. My father cut the toes out of the shoes to make room for my toes that curled. But the rags hide them in the open-toed shoes.

I looked back to the story of Mephibosheth, son of Jonathan, who was the son of Saul.

I looked at my sisters' bare feet. That's how toes were supposed to look—like the heads of children lined up in bed.

At times, we were allowed to play cards. We used them as swords. We were competitive. We were ruthless. Our mother knew this, and did not correct. I always lost to Samuel, John and Charles, but Samuel spent most of his time as an usher at Westminister. I had a better chance against my sisters.

Sometimes there was a Brussels sprout in the garden. I took the basket from the hook at the backdoor and went to look. There was largeness in the world when I stepped outside the rectory. How confining the dimness of the rooms. I hardly realized it when I was in the house. Outside, the sky was overcast, but I felt the brightness. I had to shut my eyes for a moment. Too much reading in my father's study. I hoped that heaven always was outside. I wanted to tell the family we should come out more often, but they did not want to hear anything from me.

From the garden, I heard the rattling of my mother's piano in the parlor. John and Charles, my brothers, were singing.

I looked among the leaves for a sprout, but none was there. Brussels sprouts grow on a tall stalk. When the stalk is full, the little heads are like the heads of too many children. There were some new buds toward the top of the stalk. If the sprouts were picked too soon, they were tough and bitter when boiled. They looked like cabbage heads, smaller than the heads of pygmies in Africa in one of my father's books. Soon the Brussels sprouts would be bigger and I could pick them. For now, the buds were small as my mother's thimble. I cut a few leaves from the stalk. The servant would boil them for supper and serve them with beef or pigeon or snipe. Often the leaves were covered with plant lice. I washed them at the well in the backyard, pumping the handle until a stream of water ran out. Or I picked off the lice with my fingers. Sometimes Patty and Kezzie helped.

Brussels sprouts are not like the vegetables that have to be pulled from the ground covered with dirt.

My list of longings—

> That I would not have fallen.
> That I would not have to conjugate the word fall falling fallen.
> That I would go to Oxford.
> That I would go to London.
> That I would go to the stars in their distance.

Soon John and Charles were at Oxford also. Samuel, my oldest brother, always was away. What would it be like to be one of the privileged ones? Being a sister was like climbing the steep and narrow stairs to our third-storey room.

One morning I was in the girls' room alone. Maybe my younger sisters went to the market with my mother, and she forgot to ask me. I slow them when I'm with them. But now I was alone in the room. I was by myself. Who was myself? A disfigured girl with a pleasant face. Not plain like some of my sisters. I was alone. When had I been alone? Except in the garden. Except in my father's study sometimes looking through his books. I had been alone before, but hadn't known it. How often would I be alone as my sisters were married and the boys stayed with their friends and their studies at Oxford? Who would I talk to? What would I say to myself as the only one in the room? I looked at my hands. My feet. My dress. I looked at the room I had not noticed. It was alone as I was. The bed. The cot at the foot of the bed. The wooden boards of the floor that warped in places. The wood slats on the ceiling that held up the thatch. The empty wardrobe. The little table by the bed that held a candlestick. The simple walls. The dimness. Dullness, rather. I remembered a picture had been on the wall—before one of the fires that burned the rectory. What had it been? A girl? Cross-stitched by one of my sisters? I couldn't remember. I hadn't paid attention to it.

Outside the window of the girls' room, a large white cloud lifted up a fist. I saw bees in the garden. What kind of pistol would shoot bees?

Maybe I would sit in the room alone until the Lord came for me. Was I ready? No, I would tell Him to wait until I was through shooting the bees.

Now my father looks at the horse in the book of Job. He wants an illustration of a horse for his work on Job. He wants other illustrations. And maps. John Whitelamb, a poor friend of my brothers from Lincoln College is chosen as a reader.

Hast thou given the horse strength? Has thou clothed his neck with thunder?—Job 39:19. Canst thou make him afraid as a grasshopper? The glory of his nostrils is terrible—Job 39:20.

John Whitelamb looks at John Cole's illustrations for my father's work on Job.

At first, I watch him as I slowly passed the door of the study. He does not see me. Once, I nearly trip on the edge of the floor in the hallway, and hold to the wall. The builders did not lay the floor properly after the fire, and in places, the edges of the boards lift, almost unperceptively.

John Whitelamb looks up. He smiles at me. He keeps looking. I am Molly, I tell him.

He stands. Comes to the door. He asks me into my father's messy study. I follow him to the table. At first, he does not see that I am crippled.

Afterwards, I often sit at the table while he works. Now he knows I am lame. He asks me what happened and I tell him. When he is at Oxford, he sends letters to my father inquiring about me.

John Whitelamb visited us at Epworth again and again. He asked me to sit with him while he worked.

Acts 2:21—Whosoever shall call on the name of the Lord shall be saved. Are you saved, Mary? John Whitelamb asked as I sat at the table with him.

I have heard of the Savior all my life, I answered.

He continued to read from Acts. You will not leave my soul in hell, neither will you suffer your Holy One to see corruption. You have made known to me the ways of life; you shall make me full of joy with your countenance—Acts 2:27–28. The passage was taken from Psalm 16:10–11, John Whitelamb said. King David, in all his might, knew agony also.

I felt some hard place in me dislodge. It was provoked out of its place by the words John Whitelamb read. You will not leave my soul in hell. He was working on a sermon for one of his classes. I felt the melting of the glacier that had covered the mean place in me. My family had ridiculed me. They had seen my suffering and chose to mock me. They jeered at the crippled way I walked. The misshapen legs and feet. The struggle to be one of them when they were far ahead. All of them had legs that walked. You would think they would slow and turn back and pull me along. Or find me another stick when I grew taller. Or encourage me to follow behind them at the distance I had to walk. Sometimes one of the sisters did. But mostly, they taunted me. Made fun of me. I felt sometimes they would have set me in the pasture with the cows, but the villagers would have stopped them. Maybe I should place myself there. I remembered the times my sisters had gone somewhere. Probably running in the pasture beyond our mother's gaze. I only slowed the game. It was too painful to watch them from our third-storey window. They made little noise, but I knew they were cheering over their freedom. They were running and I could not walk. I laid my head on the bed and thought of God who made everyone but me.

Jesus was rendered helpless on the cross, John Whitelamb told me as I sat with him. I felt Jesus with me. Somehow it didn't matter to him that I couldn't walk. But it mattered to me.

I looked at the Bible opened on the table before John Whitelamb. A palm tree was rising out of it. A flock by night. A Savior. Dust from a road where a donkey passed. My thoughts knew no bounds. But soon, John Whitelamb was back at Lincoln College in Oxford.

I called my servant and he gave me no answer.

—JOB 19:16.

Verses Shuffled Together Turned Out in Different Light by Mary Wesley, 1726, 29 years of age, crippled daughter of Samuel Wesley, minister, who spent his life writing the *Dissertationes in Librum Jobi*—

I had felt a light when I worked with John Whitelamb.

I felt a darkness as I sat with my father in his study. But it was in books, not men, where my life was lifted. But John Whitelamb. John Whitelamb. But books. Books, I thought. The secret life of books. There was a tower in books. A fishtrap. A river. Books made the ordinary significant. They were recognition of connections. They poked holes in the impenetrable. They pursued meaning. They told me of a world I could not reach, but knew was there because of books. They were brothers who did not leave. They were sisters who did not ask me to do their sewing. Books were my friends. They had to stay in their places. Sometimes I thought I heard their voices. I was in league with books. They were my husband. I could have many. I loved the wicked thought.

Thou hast clothed me O Lord with Vanishment. And feet turned inward. No man would ever look. I am simple. Or so my mother has said. She sits as God in our blessed house blessed with trials. I shiver under the thin covers in bed with my sisters. They strave to push me out. What obsolete words come from my thoughts. I cannot overcome them with more familiar words. The Book of Job reads like a story with its conflict and resolution. I have not denied the words of the Holy One—Job 6:10. I am blameless—Job 9:21. You know I am not guilty—Job 10:7. There is no daysman between us who might lay his hand on both—Job 9:33. Then there is the uncovered. The untrothed. Make me understand I have erred—Job 6:24. Therein, the pumping of the story. The straving to push the culprit out of his interior. And redress.

Job is considered among the oldest books of the Bible. He divides the sea—Job 26:12. If written before the crossing of the Red Sea, which came later, how did Job know? Or the writer of the Book of Job. Was the time-warp one of the opponents of trust? One of the inscrutables in the book. Insurmountables. O there is the complaint again. The arrows of the almighty are within me—Job 6:4. By the great force of my disease is my garment changed: it binds me about as the collar of my coat—Job 30:18.

My father studies the Bible. I wait for him to notice I sit beside him. He calls his work scholarship. But it is conjecture it seems to me. Guessing what Job is about. Who wrote. And where Uz is.

My welfare is passed away as a cloud—Job 30:15. I went mourning without the sun. I am a brother to dragons, and a companion to owls—Job 30:28–29. [He] scare[s] me with dreams, and terrif[ies] me through vision—Job 7:14. The chair-legs in the study bend. The table is swift. A rafter falls and skews to the floor. I wake. My father does not notice I startle. He continues his work. A rift in the man who is incomplete in his assessment, but nonetheless shriffs. In my flesh I shall see God. Whom I shall see for myself, and mine eyes shall behold, and not another—Job 19:26–27.

Where is the change in my life? Was it always in pages floating in the book? I wanted to write my thoughts between the verses in Job. I wanted to combine verses in different ways. I wanted to turn them over and watch their shadows.

Job, the defender of self. His character had not changed as yet. I was eyes to the blind, and feet to the lame. I was father to the poor, and the cause which I knew not I searched out. I broke the jaw of the wicked, and plucked the spoil out of his teeth. They waited for me as for the rain. I sat chief, and dwelt as a king in the army, as one that comforted mourners—Job 29:15–25. But now they hold me in derision whose fathers I would have disdained to set with the dogs of my flock—Job 30:1. There is the NUB OF PRIDE in Job! The dross from the force field of the human will. The crisis point. The crux. The crutch. Make me understand I have erred—Job 6:24.

All this was in the foreshadowing—I am blameless—Job 9:21. But yet Job is not. The premise has to be overturned in a story to be a story.

Was there a letter from John Whitelamb? I wanted to ask my father as he scribbled his notes. Would he go look? All the books were watching me. Their bindings turned to me. How could they see? But they did. I was tired. I was tired. I struggled not to fall asleep again, or to be caught daydreaming. Often my thoughts wandered past the heavy furniture in my father's study. The heavy drapes. But Job continued his tirade. For want and famine they were solitary [the ones who held him in derision]; fleeing into the wilderness in former time desolate and waste. Who cut up mallows by the bushes, and juniper roots for their meat. They were driven from among men to dwell in the cliffs of the valleys, in caves of the earth, and in the rocks. Among the bushes they brayed; under the nettles they were gathered together. They were children of fools, yea, children of base men: they were viler than the earth. And now I am their song, yea, I am their byword—Job 30:3–9.

There must have been gypsies in Uz. Or outcasts of some kind—or the unwanted—or families like us for the conflict and crisis of the story. My father wondered if gypsies were the lost tribes of Israel. If they were the sons of Cain, whose punishment was to wander after he killed Abel. Or the gypsies were the progeny of Ishmael. My father had long discussions with my brothers, and sometimes with John Whitelamb when he came.

Sometimes as I sat with my father, I envisioned all the books and papers going up in flames again—but they did not.

In the rectory, my wicked feet cause trouble. They complain and cramp. I sit so long I can hardly stand when I rise from the chair. My back hurts too. I follow my father to the kitchen to eat. My mother returns without meat pies. The merchant would not give her credit. We were too far in debt. We eat bread soaked in milk from our cows in the pasture, and return to the study. I find scriptures I read to my father. He looks to the ends of the earth, and sees under the whole heaven; To made weight for the winds; and he weighted the waters—Job 28:24–25.

Then the Lord answers Job out of the whirlwind—Job 38:1. Where were you when I laid the foundations of the earth?—Job 38:4. After which Job spants [a word between spout and pant]. What should I answer thee? I am vile. I will lay my hand upon my mouth—Job 40:4.

The Lord continues to speak to Job. Can you draw out leviathan with a hook? Or his tongue with a cord you let down?—Job 41:1. Can you fill his skin with barbed irons? Or his head with fish spears?—Job 41:7. His scales are shut up together with a close seal—Job 41:15. He beholds all high things: he is king over all the children of pride—Job 41:34. Thus Job, uncovered, stands before the Lord and says, I have heard of thee by hearing of the ear: but now my eye sees you—Job 42:5. Which leans toward the denouement.

Hetty, my younger sister, ran off with a lawyer who did not marry her. She returned to the parsonage and was living in Epworth in shame and misery. My father soon married her to William Wright, a brutish plumber who drank and caused her grief, and looked away from her suffering. Bless Hetty. Bless us all in our misery of marriage and lack thereof. I should consider myself fortunate that no man asked me to marry. Though thoughts of John Whitelamb buzzed in my head.

My brothers, John and Charles, continued at Oxford. My father was further in debt paying for their education. Young men came and went at our house. Emily had a friend, and I hoped she would forget Leybourne AFTER ALL THIS TIME, but after an argument, the friend was gone, and Emily was alone again. There were times in her sorrow, I could see the smallpox scars on her face. One especially on her chest she covered with a scarf. People are scarred, Emily, I told her—worse than you. Nearly everyone on the street. In the rectory, I am the unheard. The unknown. I hear my sisters come and go. I hear my mother's voice in another room. I pick at a thread on my dress. I stare eye-level at my father's desk. What am I supposed to do? I flee to thee O Lord in my trials.

These are the voices as I sit in my father's study by myself—when he is gone—maybe to walk on the road by himself—to think. I hear the voice of Job. The voice of my doubt. My intowardness.

In my father's study, I see there is no letter from John Whitelamb. I read my brothers' letters from Oxford to see if there is mention of him, but there is not.

In my father's study, I pretend I am in college.

My father has a book in his study, *Homeric Centones*, in both Greek and Latin, that he said used lines of Homer to interpret the life of Jesus. It was by a woman. A WOMAN. Eudocia. 401–460.

I pretend I am in a class. I am hearing a lecture. No, I am GIVING a lecture. It is on the cento.

A cento is made of reused words from other texts. Rehashed. Unstewed. The cento in Latin means a patchwork. A stitching. I find that on my own. There are variables in a cento. A frantic tussle. Voices collide. I feel I am separated from reason. Both narrator and character. No, the daysman has come. The daysman—our shield and buckler. Against whom the worries come with their INFUSIONS OF HURT unto me.

I ask questions of the class. I answer questions until my mother hears me talking in my father's study, and I receive a STERN lecture on talking to myself.

Questions I would ask the Lord—

> Why did the servant fall?
>
> Why was I in her arms when she fell?
>
> Was I struggling away from her when she miss-stepped?
>
> What was the purpose of the fall?
>
> Why was I the fallen?—The throw-away. At least to my family.
>
> What would I have missed if I had been whole?
>
> Is it the wounding that makes me seek You, Lord?
>
> It was Jacob who limped because he wrestled with the angel until he received a blessing—Genesis 32:26. What is my blessing?
>
> When do I think of You, Lord, that doesn't have to do with my wounding?
>
> Will I choose the pattern You give me, Lord? What other choice do I have?
>
> Will I be as relentless as the wounding?
>
> Am I someone who will receive Your grace in abundance because I suffered wounding?
>
> In the afterlife, will I have bees for toes?

I am crazy at times with thoughts of the Lord.

I am crazy at times with thoughts of John Whitelamb. He seems to want to be with me when he comes to the rectory to work for my father. Once he took my arm to help me around a chair. The chair my Uncle Matthew Wesley sent from London after the last fire so my father would have furniture in his study. My mother's brother, Samuel Annesley, of the East India Company in Surat, India, was supposed to bring her money also. A RELEASE FROM DEBT was coming. But my mother went to the wharf, and her brother was not on the ship when it came into the harbor. She never knew what happened. Why he or the money disappeared. Mystery. Mystery in the working of things. My mother kept her disappointment to herself, though it rustled like mice when I walked into the barn. Though it rusted like a door-hinge.

Do not interrupt, my father says when I make a comment. But I must be imperative. Thinking only is. But feeling also a fact of suffering. The Lord holds a candlestick. The recurring darkness is probed. What perifidy is found. Perfidy—rather. Under [the earth] it is turned up as a fire—Job 28:5. The chairs with their stray legs. All found anew. The daughters of Job coming forthwith in place of the former ones. The sons replaced. The animals. A story of restitution. Pulled with struggle from afar. Maintained in literature throughout. I only am escaped alone to tell thee—Job 1:15, 16, 17, 19. I [only] am escaped by the skin of my teeth—Job 19:20.

Now John Whitelamb and I make a study of Job. My father has worked on the book since I can remember, I tell John Whitelamb. When the papers burned in the fires, he started into them again. I remember the clump of pages curled at the edges. Blackened by soot and smoke.

John Whitelamb asks me to read some of the verses. My voice is unsure. Tense.

The arrows of the almighty are within me.

—JOB 6:4.

I feel my voice quiver. I don't want my thoughts or feelings to show. My thoughts are frightening. At night, struggling between my sisters, I am afraid. I wonder if Job had nightmares. If death scared him. Worse, if living as though dead had occurred to him. I thought maybe it had. I knew John Whitelamb was poor. My brothers had bought him a college robe when he had none. Poverty was a terror when studied directly.

What are you thinking, Mary? John Whitelamb asked during another visit.

How much the Savior likes our praises. How it makes him feel it was worth it on the cross. He could see the GLORY beyond the nailings. That is where he lives. And we live with him when we praise him.

John Whitelamb took my hand. I thought I would sob.

In bed I look at walls. I see the bumps of warts and scars. I am weary of being with myself. There is no one when I reach out my hand. Except when I think of John Whitelamb. I have to climb the stairs in the afternoon to rest in bed as shadows move across the wall. I hear the voice of the servants in the kitchen. I hear one of them call from the backdoor. I hear my mother talking to whatever sister is at work with her. Her voice is an occupant of the house. Once in a while, I hear the quick voice of a child that passes in the street. What goes by slower than a day?

I return to my father's library when I wake from sleeping. There is no other place in the house to stay out of the way. There is sleeping that is not sleep, but leaving the house in imagination, which my mother also warns against. In thought I can go where I want. Thoughts do not have legs and crippled feet. The only crippling is when there is not enough education to know the places there are to go. I thought again of teaching. But how would I get to school? How could I stand before a class?

More than once, John Wesley went to the bursar's office to make amends for John Whitelamb, who lived on almost nothing. Often my father would not pay him. Did not have the money to pay him. If my father had been able to pay him for his work, it would have gone to the bursar.

It was reported to us that someone had heard John Whitelamb say, the ungrateful Wesleys, though my brothers had bought him a robe.

Here I stop to interject a passage as I have stopped before— another book in my father's study—this one from the diary of a theologian, George Fox [1624–1691], who died five years before I was born.

> As I was walking with several friends, I lifted up my head, and saw three steeple-house spires, and they struck at my life. I asked them what place that was? They said, Lichfield. Immediately the word of the Lord came to me, that I must go thither. Being come to the house we were going to, I wished the friends to walk into the house,

saying nothing to them whither I was to go. As soon as they were gone I stept away, and went by my eye over the hedge and ditch till I came within a mile of Lichfield; where, in a great field, shepherds were keeping their sheep. Then was I commanded by the Lord to pull off my shoes. I stood still, for it was winter: but the word of the Lord was like a fire in me. So I put off my shoes, and left them with the shepherds; and the poor shepherds trembled, and were astonished. Then I walked on about a mile, and as soon as I was got within the city, the word of the Lord came to me again, saying: Cry, 'Wo to the bloody city of Lichfield!' It being market day, I went into the market-place, and to and fro in the several part of it, and made stands, crying as before, Wo to the bloody city of Lichfield. And no one laid hands on me. As I went thus crying through the streets, there seemed to me to be a channel of blood running down the streets, and the market-place appeared like a pool of blood. When I had declared what was upon me, and felt myself clear, I went out of the town in peace; and returning to the shepherds gave them some money, and took my shoes of them again. But the fire of the Lord was so on my feet, and all over me, that I did not matter to put on my shoes again, and was at a stand whether I should or no, till I felt freedom from the Lord to do so: then, after I had washed my feet, I put on my shoes again. After this a deep consideration came upon me, for what reason I should be sent to cry against that city, and call it the bloody city! For though the parliament had the minister one while, and the king another, and much blood had been shed in the town during the wars between them, yet there was no more than had befallen many other places. But afterwards I came to understand, that in the Emperor Diocletian's time a thousand Christians were martyr'd in Lichfield. So I was to go, without my shoes, through the channel of their blood, and into the pool of their blood in the market-place, that I might raise up the memorial of the blood of those martyrs, which had been shed above a thousand years before, and lay cold in their streets. So the sense of this blood was upon me, and I obeyed the word of the Lord.

I read his words again. I knew what he meant. I still heard the cows that were stabbed in the field. I wondered if the streets in Epworth would carry the sound of my limping, or our family's struggles, though we weren't martyred, or hadn't been as yet. Sometimes I felt there were enough parishioners against my father, they could form a group and come to the rectory at night and take our lives. I think that fear was the cause of some of my nightmares.

Sukey, my next oldest sister, married Richard Ellison, who was a landowner. She thought she would escape the poverty of our family, and she did. But he was a cruel man, who ended up beating her. My brothers wrote letters about it. My father did nothing.

I visited my married sisters, Sukey and Hetty. Sometimes. Not often. If there was a carriage or wagon going that way. I was more of a burden than a help when I visited. I was more burdened when I returned to Epworth than when I left. Hetty had lost several infants. She blamed the lead fumes from the furnace in William Wright's [her husband's] plumbing shop.

> Should God give and take away another [child], I can never escape the thought that my father's intercession might have prevailed against His wraith, when I shall then take to be also manifest. Forgive me, sir . . . But as you planted my matrimonial bliss so you cannot run away from my prayer when I beseech you to water it with a little kindness. My brothers will report to you what they have seen of my way of life and my daily struggle to redeem the past. But I have come to a point where I feel your forgiveness to be necessary to me. I beseech you then not to without it.
>
> —A LETTER TO SAMUEL WESLEY, HER FATHER,
> FROM MEHETABEL [HETTY] WESLEY WRIGHT

Sukey eventually left Ellison, and returned to our family with her four children. I rocked them. Sat on the back step while they played—reminding them not to shout. Be quiet or Susanna Wesley would get them. Nonetheless, they made noise. Once again, the room sounded like a colony of bees.

I sat with the servant as she folded laundry. I sat beside the servant and dried the cups and tableware she handed me. I read to Sukey's children. I looked from the window of the rectory. I called to the sky.

My Sermons—[Destroyed cruelly by my mother. Nothing original was to come from us—nothing from the daughters anyway. We were to be copies of Christian women with the starch washed out of them.]

I cry to you, O Lord, my deliverer. Woe from the bloody field of the Wesley's. I hear it cry out like George Fox heard the battlefield at Lichfield.

I cannot keep my mind on my sermons. They bleed into my Letters to Paradise. I will write my thoughts, O Lord. I cannot do what I want. I cannot. I cannot. I will tire you with my longings. I will torment you with my cries. I cannot walk. I cannot run. I cannot climb stairs. I cannot descend the stairs with the clamor of my sisters until our mother shouts at them to step lightly. She is not washed of starch.

Hear my petitions, O Lord. My repetitions. Does the wild ass bray when he hath grass? Or loweth the ox over his fodder?—Job 6:5. Give me respite and I will be silent. O Lord. O God. I think of John Whitelamb.

O that I might have my request; and that God would grant me the thing that I long for—Job 6:8.

Where is the paper on which to write? Wrapped from the butcher? My words running among the blood. The scraps of paper from my father's study? There are papers everywhere. Where does he get them? My brethren have dealt deceitfully as a brook—Job 6:15. I want to write more as I read.

When my mother destroys my sermons, it is the paper I regret, more than the words.

You preached on Sunday afternoons when father was in debtor's prison—when a locum was not handy, I say to her in an angry tempest. She is as amazed as I am at the outburst.

They are your father's words I read, she answered quickly. Not the silliness of my own thoughts. Or the irreverence. She did not slap me as she would have in the past, but I felt her words as though she had.

1727—My brother, John, came to Epworth to work in my father's church. He helped with the preaching. He visited parishioners.

1728—My brother, John, was ordained a priest.

At sundry times, in diverse manners—Hebrews 1:1. I saw the multiplicity of time moving slow—then fast—and sometimes it seemed out of order. Enlarging the night and the day. Or time shrinking until I hardly realized it passed. What day? What month? Sometimes time seemed far apart. Sometimes time stayed together.

I saw the multiplicity of the worlds—along with the multiplicity of time—the moveable worlds moving—between hope and despair—the hope of faith—the despair of reason. There were Whigs and Torys. Anglicans and Dissenters. Men and women. The world I saw and the world of Old Jeffrey, the ghost, that I could not see, who finally disappeared as we no longer heard him, unless he was asleep in a corner of the attic. Surely thinking about all of that would keep me busy.

There was the world in my father's Latin. The world in my father's Greek. The world in English. All the languages. Even the worlds inside my sisters' heads beside me on the pillow as they mumbled dichotomies. All the willows. All the birds. All the bindings. Separated in our own worlds. As the bones in my feet weren't always connected to one another, though they were in the same foot. But if my feet were crippled, my thoughts could walk.

I think of the determination of love. Who can reason with it? What if John Whitelamb asked me to marry him? I soared. What if he did not? I sank. But if he did not, I would be spared. But I did not wish to be spared. I wanted to know the channels of blood in the streets of Lichfield.

In my despair, I called out to my family. But they were occupied and didn't hear. Or if they heard, no one would come. How could there be such solitude in the crowded, thorny nest of the rectory? Yet I had to think how life moved on in a generous way.

I was alone in the world. Yet John Whitelamb, on his next visit, spoke to me quietly in my father's study. He said he felt we should be married. I felt a lump rise in my throat. He would eventually speak to my father. Not now. Not at this moment. But sometime. When he left, I climbed the stairs and stood in the upstairs window of the girls' room. I knew John Whitelamb would come for me and take me away from the rectory. I would step from the third-storey window when he came, and he would catch me.

Charles, my brother, on his next visit from Oxford, informed me that John Whitelamb had another friend, a young woman, in Medley. Miss Betty. I was devastated as I listened. I was thrown down the stairs once again. Crippled in another way. I gulped a barn-full of air. I stood up. No, I was happy. It would save me from a disappointing marriage. John Whitelamb was an indigent scholar. I had enough of poverty. No, I was not happy. I was crushed. I acted like it didn't make any difference. The impossible had happened, then was ripped away. I didn't tell Charles that John Whitelamb had nearly asked me to marry him. I didn't want my brother to have something else to torment me with. I read the book of Job again. Suffering as he suffered. This was the agony Emily felt with Leybourne—and my older sisters felt with their husbands. Why were we destined only for what would harm us?

Soon, I was sick with an illness. I did not know what it was. I lay in a delirium in our bed until my mother moved me to my brothers' vacant room. People wandered here and there with nowhere to go. I could hear them in the room. They were trapped in their thoughts. They could not get out. They were unable to reach the light of God they knew was somewhere above them. The world outside faith terrified me. I didn't want to be one of them. I would believe. I would believe. NO MATTER WHAT.

What is the cause of nightmares? A sister [Anne] playing the trumpet [not well]. The trumpet becoming a serpent that crawled across the floor and up the bed post and under the covers. The sound of it crawling through my ears into my head. I was in bed by myself—the bees were striking in the field. They were a mob at the door reaching with the roots of flowers into a crevice of the garden walk. I walked on a street turned to water and a boat could not be found. I woke in a start reaching for the oar of my sister, but there was a field of blood—and no one to bring me home. I waited for the serpent that would take me.

My Letters to Paradise—
For some there is no magic. For some there is only bee stings. For some there is no song. Only the words of faith. There will be a place where recompense is made. He shall send Jesus Christ who before was preached unto you, whom the heavens must receive until the restitution is made—Acts 3:20–21. Though we are sick, you heal us. Though we are lame, you cause us to walk. Or will walk. [The Lord heals. Only be patient.] Meanwhile, we crawl along the floor. When my feet hurt, I got downstairs by sitting on one step and lowering myself to the next. There are times my legs jump and wake me from trying to sleep.

There are stars in the sky. Cows in the field. The sisters breathing and turning in our bed. Patty's leg in my back. Kezzie's elbow against my ribs. Sometimes a rodent in the thatch of the roofing. I know sometimes they run across the floor.

Love is darkness that cannot be seen until you are in it. Love is a lame foot. Spare me from love. Emily still cries over Leybourne. How long will she pine? Not because our oldest brother, Samuel, discouraged him in front of our mother, but because Leybourne didn't appear and prove them wrong. Three years Emily wrote to him and received his letters. Three years and they weren't married. It was time to know it would not be him. Time to grieve over him for always. That ugly smallpox scar permanent on her chest.

Emily's love could not be forgotten. Ever or ever. Though I sorrow over Whitelamb, I am satisfied to have no one who would cause that kind of pain, I keep telling myself, as I see Emily sorrow over Leybourne as I sorrow over the limitation of my feet.

I saw the marriages of Hetty and Sukey turn dismal over the years. I saw the deaths of some of their newborns. I knew I would see the marriages of younger sisters yet to take place. I would see the death of more newborns in the family.

I return to the book of Job again and again by myself. I cry unto thee, and thou dost not hear me: I stand up, and thou regardest me not. Thou art become cruel to me: with thy strong hand thou opposes thyself against me. Thou liftest me up to the wind; thou causest me to ride upon it, and dissolvest my substance—Job 30:21–23.

This is why my sister cried. This is what it is to have a burden in the heart. But I rode on the wind. Until I was nothing seen from earth. Nothing. In that, maybe there is rest.

1728—I was at the table one afternoon with Kezzie, the youngest sister, when two men carried my father, limping, into the rectory. He walked the way I walked.

What happened? Kezzie cried.

Forgive me, Lord, I always think of myself first. How tattered Your thoughts must be of me. Forgive my fretful ways.

I listened to my father—

The horse stumbled. My father fell, catching one foot in the stirrup. The horse dragged him, stepping also on his other leg, but my father was spared!

I'm sore, but not hurt, he said. The Lamb of God had interceded. We are held in a hard but merciful world.

The two men looked at him. My mother looked at him, and all were amazed that there was no injury other than bruising and soreness.

If hymns came from me as they did Charles, I would sing praises.

I sat on the back step of the rectory with my fourth sister, Anne. She had taken off her shoes to sun her feet. I looked at her feet, studying the way toes were supposed to be. I saw the tree branches in the sky over the barn and the houses on the lane in the distance. My toes were like branches going everywhere. My feet were trees standing on the horizon wherever they were taken by the will. Anne's toes could walk. It was my feet that were like the trees rooted to the ground that would stay in one place. What a strange and unfair place—the world.

How often we were called upon to pass through the fire.

1729—John returned to Oxford and and founded the Oxford Methodists. He talked with Moravians of going to America—to Georgia—to establish a mission among the Indians.

What were Oxford Methodists? Where did he get the idea? Probably from our mother who ran the rectory that way. I could form a Methodist Club among the sisters. God required more of girls. Confined to houses with thoughts of husbands instead of ideas like men thought. We could run through the house with fire in our ears. Maybe I could ask John to join his Oxford Methodist Club. Was I not devout? What did I do that would displease him? Other than complain with bitterness. But in the middle was a longing for the Lord. Maybe it meant a longing to be out of the rectory. To be at Oxford. To walk on feet that walked. To talk about ideas of holiness. Why exactly were they? How could one be holy inside human bones? I saw the flaws of my brothers and my father. I could tell them the areas in themselves they needed to address. They could tell me mine. We could have discourse. We could read scripture and discuss it. I would like that rather than being told about it. What did it mean? In what ways could it be interpreted? Could we discuss it as we did Virgil and Homer? Or was it something that belonged to God only and we had to leave it alone? Thinking about scripture lifted my spirit though often it was heavy. Or I seemed to think it was. Often it was about suffering, patience and tolerance. Or it seemed to me that way.

Now my father was in peril again.

I was at the table with Kezzie when we heard the rumbling of a cart in front of the rectory. Once again, two men carried my father. This time, John Whitelamb followed. Kezzie was mending and stuck her finger with the needle. I was struck with awkwardness when I saw him again. It was too late to leave the room. It would be more awkward if I tried. I would have to limp in front of him. The men told us our father was on the Burringham Ferry when it tucked underwater. John Whitelamb had saved my father.

We tried to get the story straight—A storm came across the water, John told us—fierce enough that their horses were thrown overboard by the wind. John Whitelamb and my father held on. But soon, John said—they realized the boat was taking on water. John Whitelamb took ahold of my father as they went into the river. He held onto him in the turbulence, and dragged him to shore. The mares swimming ahead of them.

John Whitelamb. I repeat his name too often. Mr. Whitelamb. No—John Whitelamb.

Though my father was stingy with money, he afterwards helped John Whitelamb at Lincoln College in Oxford. He paid him what he owed him for his work.

Kezzie. Kezzie. I thought I would never see him again.

If I could be quiet. If I could be still. If my thoughts would rest.

Where is a book written the way my thoughts fly? There—in Psalm 91. It was difficult to get into because it was like following my own thoughts that came like a flock of birds, landing then lifting from the field, flying to various trees, lifting again and shifting directions mid-air suddenly and gracefully as if clothes blowing in the wind. The servant hurrying to take the pieces of clothing from the line in a sudden drizzle. If it weren't for my feet, I would have other thoughts. If it weren't for poverty. Dresses and ribbons and the young men that came to the rectory in Epworth with my brothers.

Thine

> Because thou hast made the Lord, which is my refuge, even the most High, thy habitation.
>
> —PSALM 91:9

To memorize is work. To memorize Psalm 91 is more work. How many involved?—God, and the narrator, and the you to whom the narrator speaks? And who wrote?—Moses? David? Or someone who rolled, *you*, *he*, *I*, and *me*, like flames? Nonetheless, Psalm 91 is fortress and refuge against plague, pest, lion, adder, dragon. It takes thee [me] into heaven.

Memory work in a hard time is harder work. You [me] with broken feet and a sore back and others reeved up with uncertainty. All of it having to do mostly with husbands for the sisters. And me pining quietly after one also—namely John Whitelamb. But in the psalm, a broken text breaks open with feathers, wings, and tenuous shadows. There is light in whatever darkness befalls. The angels themselves hold thee [me] up in their hands, while ten thousand fall at my right hand.

Outside, there is storm. The trees themselves waver in the wind, more messengers than landscape. The sheltering words unfold the horizon of heaven. The narrator speaks. The noisome pestilence shall not come nigh thy [my] dwelling. So exuberant the promise of the narrator, the voice of God himself [or so it seems] interrupts. Because he has set his love on me, I will deliver him. I will set him on high. I will be with him in trouble. I will deliver him—from 91:14–15.

I see David trying to stay warm in the cold—blowing on his fingers so he can write his words on animal hide. David, the provider for Mephibosheth. Or Moses in the desert with a pen on parchment, poking holes, leaving blots as he wrote. Those holy ones—all men of letters. And I, the one to whom the psalm is addressed, is memorizing words. With more needs than Moses facing the Red Sea. Or Hetty, my sister, dealing with infant mortality. Yet twice at the close, the verses say, I will deliver you. I will deliver you. And once, I will be with you in trouble.

Emily had news that an apothecary was showing her attention. She admired Uncle Matthew Wesley, and hoped maybe Robert Harper would be like him. But Uncle Matthew was a physician in London. Harper was a traveling apothecary to the poor. He didn't even have a shop in Epworth. He often was gone. I had a foreboding about him, though I didn't trouble Emily. I thought Harper would be more like Uncle Samuel Annesley, our mother's brother, whom we had hoped would alleviate some of our financial woes, but nothing came forthwith from Uncle Samuel Annesley.

The next month, I study the word, lame. They were not allowed to make an offering. A blind man, or a lame, or he who has a flat nose—Leviticus 21:18.

Or a man that is brokenfooted, or brokenhanded—Leviticus 21:19.

Or the crookbackt, or a dwarf, or that hath a blemish in this eye, or be scurvy, or scabbed—Leviticus 21:20.

What could I make of God?—in whom I believed, or tied to believe, or believed usually when I thought of Him. God was. He is. He will be. We actually had no choice in our family. We were believers. Until I read the lame were rejected in Leviticus. Faith is a battle to believe. Maybe that's why God makes it hard to believe. The whole family wrapped in armor. Trying to find a way through the muddle of faith. The interpretations of it. My father always in trouble. Those below and above him. The squat parishioners. The officials of the church. The leaders of Epworth. Even neighbors sometimes rose up against us. Was faith only what we termed it to be? A matter of nomenclature? Of naming. This is the way I believe. Rejected by God as well as family. Living was a battlefield of belief. Though I think war is fought in heaven also. The way the Bible is strung together, it could be taken to fit one's proclivity. It seemed to be a war of disagreement in itself. I found other verses for the lame.

The feet of the lame are not equal—Proverbs 26:7.

The lame take the prey—Isaiah 33:23.

The lame shall leap like a hart—Isaiah 35:6.

My father. Poor father. Suffering with gout and now palsy. Hardly able to move his pen in a steady line. There was disappointment that his study of Job had not provided income. He was misunderstood. He was ridiculed—poor Job had to bear his three friends as well as Samuel Wesley's writing about him. My father was a Pietist. I never knew his harshness, though I heard it toward others. Nor his unbending politics. I think he wanted to live in the time before all the children were born to him, and he spent his days writing, and leaving the Dissenters, and becoming a member of the established Anglican Church, and writing and writing his thoughts and philosophies. His Pietist stance. A strong man. A weak man. A wanting father. No, his influence was in Samuel, John and Charles. I was afraid they would become Dissenters and pull away from Anglicanism. He could not stop them if they did. But I knew they would not. He only could float along the surface blown here and there by unstable winds.

My mother, Susanna, often was ill. Emily mostly cared for her.

Emily, dear Emily, still pining after Robert Leybourne for years. Love seemed to be a storm that blew across fields and left rubble not of one's own in the yard. Rubble that could not be removed. Didn't I know its effectiveness? John Whitelamb had hinted of marriage, but that hint had passed.

In the meantime, Patty was in love with Westley Hall, a member of the Oxford Methodists. He visited Epworth, and decided he was in love with Kezzie. He ignored Patty for a while, and courted Kezzie, then announced that the Lord told him that Patty after all was to be his wife. Kezzie eventually went to live with them. Hall had other lovers and eventually brought one of the infants for Patty to care for, which she did. All of this, and aging parents, ever before me.

I picked some berries along the road where I hobbled. I told the servant to bake it in bread. It wasn't fruitcake, but it would be something like it. There was more than one kind of fruitcake. There was a multitude of fruitcakes.

> And it shall come to pass . . . that the Lord shall hiss [whistle or call] for the . . . bee that is in the land of Assyria.
>
> —ISAIAH 7:18

The Amorites, who dwelt in that mountain, came against you and chased you as bees do.

—DEUTERONOMY 1:44

Amorites—I called my brothers and sisters who tormented me. If not with their words, with their lives. I could not run. I could not walk. But I could sit and study my lessons, which I did not always want to do. It seemed to me life was a series of woundings I had to get through. Or a series of mishaps. Or a series of unending children. Sukey's girls often clung to me of a morning, the marks of their sleeping caps still on their foreheads. I would have to let out some of the binding, as I had done before, but then the caps fell off their heads at night.

How often my thoughts were sisters when there was nothing else. Where did they come from? They were like the thoughts in the Bible that went on and on.

One morning, I heard a voice downstairs that I knew. John Whitelamb was in Epworth—in the rectory—to do more work for my father. I stayed upstairs and would not see him when he asked.

He insisted, and my mother made me come downstairs. I did so without grace, so he could see my awkwardness and know the woman in Lincoln was more admirable.

John Whitelamb assured me he was not in love with the other woman. I should not always listen to my brother. In my father's study, John Whitelamb asked me to MARRY him. He had written to my father to ask his permission. John Whitelamb said my father had agreed. The books looked from their library shelves. They were struck. Would they fall from the shelves? The unbelievable happened. My family was aghast. I was 36 years old. He was 14 years younger than me, but I became his wife.

My Letters to Paradise—
The bee stings, but also gives honey. In the message of the Bible, there is hell in the afterlife. There also is heaven.

I saw John Whitelamb at the altar when I walked into the church at Epworth. I wore one of Emily's dresses. I carried a small sprig of holly that birds had not eaten. Anne had picked it in a clump of trees on the far edge of our pasture. I saw a blue Juniper berry and a purple pokeweed mixed with the holly. Tied with a ribbon. In the church, I saw a few of our parishioners. I stood before the altar with John Whitelamb as Pastor Horberry married us. My parents sat with a few of my sisters on the pew behind us. It was December 21, 1733. The winter solstice. St. Thomas Day. A day when poor children went house to house—*Thomasing. Mumping. Doling* for baked goods. I had wanted to go as a child. But my mother would not allow it.

After the ceremony we had tea and a dessert made of boiled wheat, milk, sugar and cinnamon. It was St. Thomas Day. Doubting Thomas. The disciple that had to touch the nail holes in the hands of Jesus before he believed. St. Thomas Day. The sister who doubted herself had married. The sister whom everyone doubted would marry had married. A few children came to the door of the rectory for a bite of the wedding dessert.

John Whitelamb and I moved to the rectory in Wrott after the marriage, a short afternoon journey from Epworth by wagon, and sometimes by boat if the water was high. The large, upright gravestones in the churchyard cemetery looked like people in the fog as we neared the church.

Sometimes we walked in the marshes, and I held to his arm. We listened to the birds that called to us. The sky widened. I was at home in the rectory. I could stay forever. I sat beside John as he wrote his sermons. I was on the front row of the church when he preached. I sang with the hymns. I stood with the servant as she hung the sheets on the line. I oversaw the household duties. My sister, Sukey, with her children, visited with news that my father fell from a wagon. He seemed frailer as time went on.

Soon, I realized I was going to have a child.

My list of concerns—

> What if I could not run to the child when it needed me?
> What would the child say when it saw my crooked feet?
> Would it try to copy the way I walked?

I was going to have a CHILD. I repeated it to myself daily as I worked in the rectory at Wrott.

Molly miraculously gets money, even in Wrott, and has given the first-fruits of her earnings to her mother, lending her money, and presenting her with a new cloak of her own buying and making—for which God will bless her.

—A LETTER FROM JOHN WESLEY

1734—I sat at the table in our small rectory beside John Whitelamb. I wrote the names for the unborn child across his sermon notes. He didn't mind. Mephibosheth Wesley Whitelamb. Phibosheth. Phillip. Mephibos. Thomas. Wesley Mephibosheth Whitelamb. Jonathan Mephibos Whitelamb. Joanna Bosheth Whitelamb. Mary Mephibosheth Whitelamb. No servant would be allowed to carry her down the stairs.

A list of what I like—

> The rectory at Wroth.
> No sisters pushing me out of bed.
> Walking the marsh in the morning.
> The sufficiency of birds.
> Walking the marsh in the evening.

Saying Psalm 91 [that I memorized] to John Whitelamb—He who dwells in the secret place of the Most High shall abide under the shadow of the Almighty—and saying to John Whitelamb, my husband, the secret place of the Most High seemed to me to be Jesus Christ—or having faith in Jesus seemed the secret place. If someone on the road passed in a cart—John Whitelamb would say, the Lord be with you. But if they did not attend church, and maybe had not heard, nor wanted to hear, they would have no idea of what John Whitelamb meant. Nor understand Psalm 91—that Jesus was a hidden place. That faith in him was.

There were a few days I stayed in bed. It seemed the rectory was a boat in the marshes of Wrott. I felt I was floating anyway. John Whitelamb chopped wood. He visited parishioners. He took the horse to be shoed. Sometimes I think he prepared the meals and carried the tray up the stairs to our bed. Soon I was able to get up and continue my duties. As the summer passed, I sat with him while he balanced church accounts. I sat beside him as he read. I knitted a little cap for the baby.

> . . . he [Samson] turned aside to see the carcass of the lion; and behold, there was a swarm of bees and honey in the carcass of the lion.
>
> —JUDGES 14:8

When the Bees Leave—
The Multiplicity of Worlds.
October, 1734—Childbirth, not a year after the wedding—

Death by childbirth. If the bees leave in the rain, they return in childbirth. I hear the drone of their wings. The muffled roar of their coming. The Lord is a Lamb. The Lord is a Bee. There is honey in his wings. There is hope in the hours of childbirth. It is not forthcoming. I thought of bee stings in my stomach. The sharp intrusions. Over and over. It was a swarm of bees. Landing. They are roaring now. Maybe it is my voice. But it is the bees. I could not roar that way. I heard poor John Whitelamb, my husband, the child's father, moaning with prayer. Pleading. His droning and the humming of the bees blurred together with the amalgamation of a fruitcake. The way there was multiplicity of longing. For a child. For a life. I saw it there in the shop window. I was tiring. I was going somewhere. I was flying on bee wings. There were more stabs.

Their stingers were blunt poles trying to poke their way into me. Or out of me. There were bees in the carcass of my belly. O Lord. Merciful Lord. I thought now. Only You are singular. Not broken into parts and avenues that go this way and that through a town. In You I will be. And Job, the whole book of suffering Job. The whole suffering book. John Whitelamb continued to plead with the Lord. Suffering. Suffering. I was weak. I hardly could lift my hand. I was baking. I wanted him to know the bees had come for the child. They were taking me to where it had gone.

Afterword

I myself become the wounded person

— Walt Whitman, "Song of Myself"

John Wesley, founder of the Methodist Church, had seven sisters. I wanted to know about the sisters because they receive little notice. When I read Frederick Maser's *Seven Sisters in Search of Love*, I was struck with Mary, who was lame in both feet. I wrote about the Wesley family from her point-of-view.

I wanted a blustery tone for Mary Wesley. She was suppressed yet passionate as she struggled for acceptance from her family, and an understanding of God who could heal all, yet left her lame. The manuscript covers Mary from her early life in the Epworth Rectory, until her death from childbirth at the age of 37. Mary speaks in a somewhat fragmented manner, as though her story is difficult to express. There also are interruptions from her family, and sometimes her own thoughts. I felt at times I was writing a crippled text. In the end, I think there is a way you can break language so that it says more than it could when it is whole.

From the beginning, I knew this was not going to be a happy story. The Wesley sisters lived in poverty. They had unhappy lives.

I started to write about Mary Wesley in the fall of 2015. On November 9, 2015, I broke my ankle. I got out of my car in the drive to look at something. I thought I had the car in park, but it must have been in reverse. When I saw the car start to roll backwards, I tried to put my foot on the brake, but the open door pushed me on the ground and the front tire ran over both legs above the knees.

My car backed on across the street where it came to a stop in a neighbor's yard. No other bone was broken.

In my years of writing historical voices that did not have a chance to speak, I've become convinced of the connection between past and present. If Mary Wesley was crippled, I would be also. I had a cast on my left ankle for six weeks. A large fracture blister broke inside the cast and left an open sore. For three months, after the cast was removed, I changed bandages twice a day until it finally closed. My feet swelled. My knees were twice their size. Some of the upper parts of my legs calcified. I went to physical therapy. I am still recovering.

At one point in the difficulties, I had the thought, I would lay down my life if I could, but it continues.

During that time, both my adult son and daughter had surgeries. It is when nothing holds together, the Lord enters the midst. I know as I have known in my long life that there is a merciful God whose grace is sufficient.